GRACIE La Roo

SETS SAIL

written by MARSHA QUALEY

illustrated by KRISTYNA LITTEN

raintree
a Capstone company — publishers for children

Raintree is an imprint of Capstone Global Library
Limited, a company incorporated in England and
Wales having its registered office at 264 Banbury
Road, Oxford, OX2 7DY – Registered company
number: 6695582

www.raintree.co.uk
yorders@raintree.co.uk

Text © Capstone Global Library Limited 2018
The moral rights of the proprietor have been asserted.

Edited by Megan Atwood
Designed by Aruna Rangarajan
Illustrated by Kristyna Litten
Production by Steve Walker
Printed and bound in China

ISBN 978 1 474 74472 0
21 20 19 18 17
10 9 8 7 6 5 4 3 2 1

British Library Cataloguing in Publication Data
A full catalogue record for this book is available from
the British Library.

CONTENTS

GRACIE and The

NAME: Gracie LaRoo

TEAM: Water Sprites

CLAIM TO FAME:
Being the youngest pig
to join a world-renowned
synchronized swimming team!

SIGNATURE MOVE:
"When Pigs Fly" Spin

LIKES: Purple, clip-on tail bows,
mud baths, new-mown hay
smell

DISLIKES: Too much attention,
doing laundry, scary films

QUOTE

"I just hope I can be the kind of synchronized
swimmer my team needs!"

WATER SPRITES

JINI

BARB

JIA

SU

MARTHA

BRADY

SILVIA

A STERN CAPTAIN

Gracie LaRoo stood at the railings on the ship and watched dolphins frolic in the ocean.

"Welcome aboard, cousin," a voice called.

Gracie spun around. "Joanna! It's so great to see you! And this cruise ship is just beautiful. Thank you so much for inviting us!"

The two cousins hugged. Then Joanna asked, "Where are the Water Sprites?"

"Still sleeping," Gracie said. "Everyone got to bed late because they were so excited. I am, too!" Then Gracie wrung her hands. "At first the Sprites weren't sure performing on this cruise was a good idea. But I convinced them we would get new fans if we did shows here!"

Suddenly Joanna's eyes got wide and she straightened up.

Gracie said, "What's wrong?"

But Joanna spoke to someone behind Gracie. "Hello, Captain," she said.

Gracie turned around.

A sow in a splendid uniform
walked up to them. She said to
Joanna, "This must be one of the
swimmers." Her voice sounded
stern and her face was serious.

Joanna nodded, and the captain continued. She looked at Gracie. "Your team has won many medals. I hope you can put on a good show. Joanna says you can. I'm putting my trust in her."

With that, the captain turned around and walked away.

Joanna turned to Gracie with wide, nervous eyes. Gracie hugged her and said, "We will make you proud! We can't wait to perform!"

CHAPTER 2

DISASTER!

Joanna showed Gracie around the ship. When they reached the top deck Joanna said, "This is where the Sprites will perform every afternoon."

Gracie was delighted. A waterslide towered above the glittering pool.

Suddenly Joanna shouted, "Stop, ma'am. The pool is not open yet!"

A sow in an orange robe was dipping a hoof in the water. She said,  "The captain told me I could have a quick dip before I taught my first class. I am Rita Sinclair."

Gracie whispered, "You didn't tell me there was a famous dancer on the ship!"

Joanna nodded excitedly. Then she said to the sow, "Miss Sinclair, I didn't recognize you. I am so sorry."

Miss Sinclair smiled and said, "Quite all right, sweetie!" Then she dropped her robe on a pool chair and dove into the water.

That afternoon the Sprites got ready as a team for their first show on the ship.

The dressing room was busy and loud.

Joanna poked her head in the door. "We're ready at the pool," she said. "The captain is there."

Her eyes got wide and Gracie
winked at her to reassure her.

As the team lined up for their
entrance walk, Gracie wished:
Please, please, please let it all be perfect!

But everything was not perfect.

Tiny piglets ran around their
legs as they entered.

Pigs booed and shouted as the

Sprites performed.

One piglet threw a beach ball

at the Wiggly Piggly Pyramid. The

Sprites fell and broke apart, belly-

flopping into the pool.

After that, the piglets thought it was funny to throw all sorts of things at the Sprites.

Gracie's triple spin was a triple tumble into the water.

When she popped back up, she saw the captain near Joanna at the side of the pool.

The captain was frowning and shaking her head.

GRACIE'S IDEA

Joanna joined the team at dinner. "I am so sorry about the show."

Barb said, "That crowd was wild and mad. They wanted to be in the pool."

Joanna said, "The captain got many complaints about the pool and waterslide being closed."

She looked near tears. "She's

afraid we might have to . . .

cancel all your performances!"

All the Sprites gasped.

"I persuaded the captain to

let you have one more chance,"

Joanna said. "But she told me

that if you don't make the crowd

happy, then you will get off the

ship at Port Wallow and go home."

"Oh, no!" said Su. "What if the news gets out that the Water Sprites failed?"

"We wanted new fans," added Martha. "Not enemies."

Gracie didn't want her friends to see her tears. She said, "I'm going for a walk."

Disaster! she thought, as she hurried away. How could she fix it?

As Gracie walked on an upper deck, thinking hard, she heard music and thumping from one of the activity rooms.

Tap dancing!

Gracie peeked into the room.

It was crowded with older

sows. At the very front, with her

back to the room, danced Rita

Sinclair.

Gracie watched and listened as the famous dancer called out steps, and the other dancers followed along. Miss Sinclair led the dancers around the room in a long line.

Gracie smiled. She had a perfect idea.

CHAPTER 4

A FABULOUS SHOW

When the class was over, Gracie slipped inside.

Miss Sinclair was talking with three of the dancers.

One of the dancers noticed Gracie, "You're one of the swimming pigs! I saw your show yesterday."

Another dancer said, "Those piglets were terrible, the way they threw things at you."

Miss Sinclair wrinkled her snout. "Piglets bothered a performer? Unacceptable!"

The third dancer said, "If my grandpigs did something like that they would be in trouble."

Gracie said, "Miss Sinclair,
you don't know me but I'm a big
fan. I've watched videos of your
Hogway shows over and over."

"How very sweet," said Miss

Sinclair, curtseying.

"And when I was watching the class," Gracie continued, "I had an idea how to make our next show go better. But I would need your help." She looked at the other dancers. "In fact, we would need all of you to help us."

The next afternoon a huge crowd waited by the pool.

"There are so many people today," Jini said to Gracie.

"Rita and her dancers certainly spread the word!" said Gracie.

When the music began, Miss Sinclair led two lines of tap-dancing sows through the crowd to the pool. At the water's edge, the lines danced apart.

There were the Water Sprites!

The dancers tapped into position all around the pool, and the Sprites dove in.

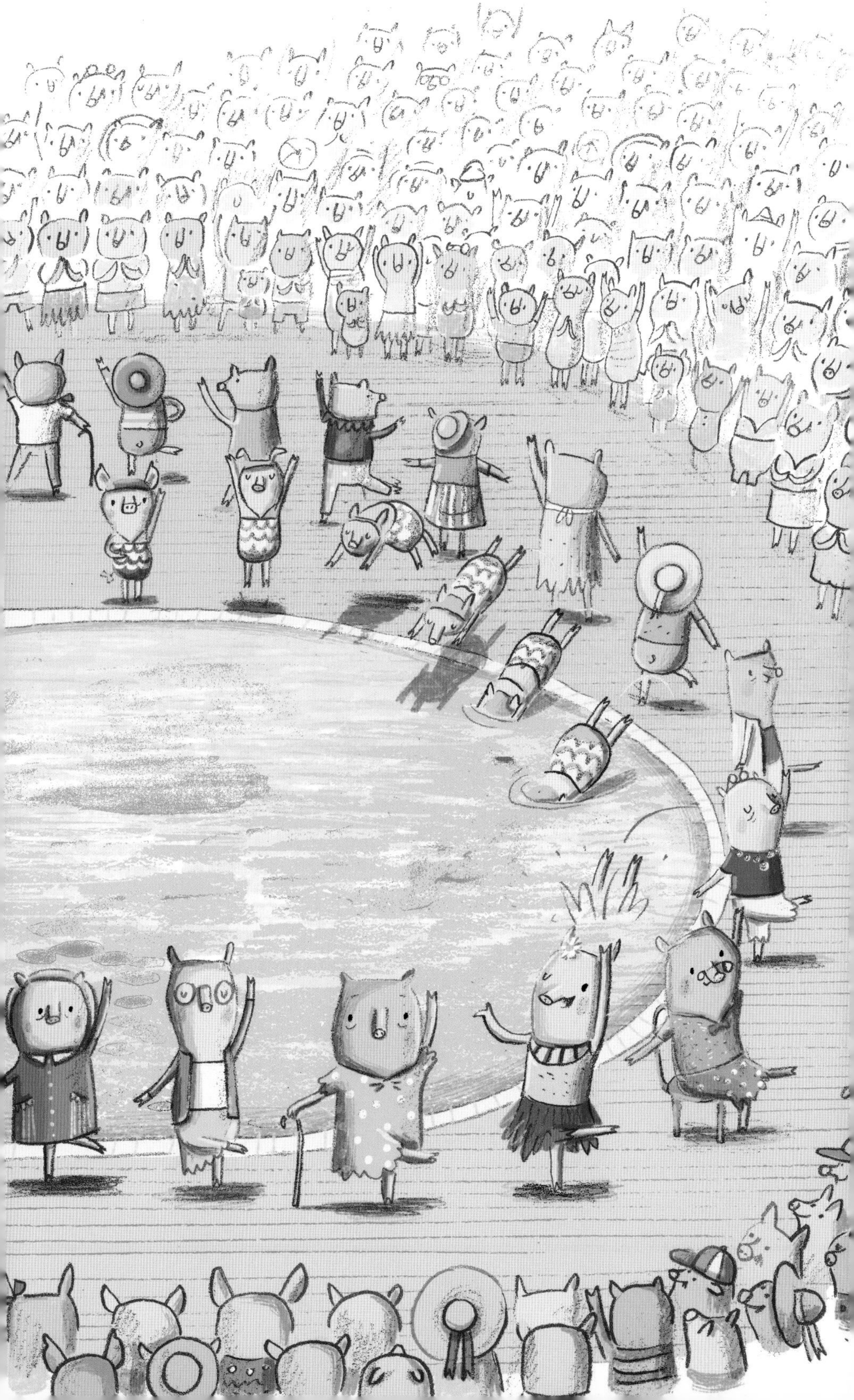

With Miss Sinclair and the
grannies on guard, no piglets
caused trouble.

With Miss Sinclair and the
grannies leading the cheers,
the crowd joined in.

The show was like a wonderful dream.

The Dolphin Arches Formation made a beautiful circle.

The Wiggly Piggly Pyramid rose high above the water.

Gracie's final spin into the pool dazzled the crowd.

When she burst back up, she heard a fresh roar of applause.

She saw piglets dancing with the sows. She saw smiling faces.

And she saw the captain hugging Joanna. She heard the captain say, "What a great idea, Joanna! How many shows can we get them to do?"

Gracie twirled happily.

GLOSSARY

belly-flop   land on your stomach

curtsey   put one foot in front of the other and bend the knees as a way of formally greeting someone; normally done by women or girls

dazzling   exciting!

frolic   run around and play

glittering   sparkling

persuade   talk someone into something

splendid   beautiful and lovely

TALK ABOUT IT!

1. The piglets on the ship were very rowdy. Have you been in a situation when kids around you were being rowdy? What did you do?

2. Why do you think the piglets calmed down when the grannies stepped in?

3. Gracie was afraid she'd put her teammates in a bad situation. Have you ever felt that way? Were you able to make the situation better?

WRITE ABOUT IT!

1. Pretend you are Gracie's cousin, Joanna. Write a letter to the captain of the ship asking if the Water Sprites could perform.

2. Write a letter from Gracie to Rita, thanking her for helping out the Water Sprites.

3. Write a story from the point of view of one of the piglets on the ship. What was it like to see the Water Sprites perform?

Marsha Qualey is the author
of many books for readers young
and old. Though she learned to
swim when she was very young,
she says she has never tried any of
the moves and spins Gracie does
so well.

Marsha has four grown-up
children and two grandchildren.
She lives in Wisconsin, USA, with
her husband and their two non-
swimming cats.

About the illustrator

Kristyna Litten is an award winning children's book illustrator and author. After studying illustration at Edinburgh College of Art, she now lives and works in Yorkshire in the UK, with her pet rabbit Herschel.

Kristyna would not consider herself a very good swimmer as she can only do the breaststroke, but when she was younger, she would do a tumble roll and a handstand in the shallow end of the pool.

THE WONDERFUL, THE AMAZING, THE PIG-TASTIC GRACIE LAROO!

Discover more at
www.raintree.co.uk

- Find out more about Gracie and her adventures.

- Follow the Water Sprites as they craft their routines.

- Figure out what you would do . . . if you were the awesome Gracie LaRoo!

Praise for *A Man Most Driven*

'Peter Firstbrook's tenacious research for *A Man Most Driven* convinces me even more that Smith's life was just as incredibly swashbuckling as Smith himself so colourfully but truthfully described.'

William M. Kelso, Director of Research and Interpretation at the Jamestown Rediscovery Project and author of *Jamestown: The Buried Truth*

'Captain John Smith's iconic shadow still falls over Jamestown 400+ years after his 34-month sojourn in helping to found it. A new and readable biography helps to brighten that shadow and add human dimensions to that icon. This is a worthy addition to anyone's library collection on Jamestown.'

First California Company, Jamestowne Society

'An assiduous researcher with a talent for cohesive narration, [Firstbrook] brushes aside the more common historian's plagues of suspect first-person accounts and competing narratives. Smith's autobiography, for instance, is the only record in many cases, but if a 10th of his bombastic tellings are true (and Firstbrook's sleuthing convincingly puts them at a much higher percentage), he still led an astonishingly adventurous life.'

***The Providence Journal*, Best Books of 2014**

'Peter Firstbrook has written a book that grabs the reader at the prologue and dangerously interferes with his sleep and his spouse's good humour as he refuses to put it down! This book will reside in an easy to find area of my shelf, for I know I will come back to it when I want to read a 'real' adventure story.'

Casey Criswell, *Journal of the Early Americas*

'A lively and vivid new exploration of an extraordinary life.'

Matthew Parker, author of *The Sugar Barons*

'A riveting account of the astonishing adventures of one of the true heroes of English and American history. This is a real page-turner and makes history truly come alive.'

beth's Spymaster
Spanish Armada

'*A Man Most Driven* goes a long way to telling the whole story of Smith not only as an American pioneer, but also a global visionary. No one would believe his life and adventures – but this book shows they're true.'

Bob Holman, poet, activist, and star of *Captain Smith Goes to Ukraine*

'A nuanced account of the English captain saved by Pocahontas reveals an astonishingly complicated personality. Exciting historical tales with romantic overtones.' *Kirkus Reviews*

'[A] thoroughly-researched biography of John Smith… With so much of Smith's life known only through his own contradictory writings, Firstbrook approaches the subject with healthy skepticism, examining just where Smith's claims might be exaggerated and where history backs them up. In the process, Firstbrook also takes a closer look at the legend of Pocahontas, at least partially debunking the motives behind her timely intervention in Smith's death sentence, suggesting that the entire episode might have been more performance on Smith's part than he originally made out… Detail-rich, drawing heavily from Smith's writings to tell the story of a larger-than-life figure with an uncanny knack for survival.' *Publishers Weekly*